The Swindler

Ethel M. Dell

"When you come to reflect that there are only a few planks between you and the bottom of the Atlantic Ocean, it makes you feel sort of pensive."

"I beg your pardon?"

The stranger, smoking his cigarette in the lee of the deck-cabins, turned his head sharply in the direction of the voice. He encountered the wide, unembarrassed gaze of a girl's grey eyes. She had evidently just come up on deck.

"I beg yours," she rejoined composedly. "I thought at first you were some one else."

He shrugged his shoulders, and turned away. Quite obviously he was not disposed to be sociable upon so slender an introduction.

The girl, however, made no move to retreat. She stood thoughtfully tapping on the boards with the point of her shoe.

"Were you playing cards last night down in the saloon?" she asked presently.

"I was looking on."

He threw the words over his shoulder, not troubling to turn.

The girl shivered. The morning air was damp and chill.

"You do a good deal of that, Mr.—Mr.—" She

paused suggestively.

But the man would
not fill in the blank.
He smoked on in
silence.

The vessel was rolling
somewhat heavily,
and the splash of the
drifting foam reached
them occasionally
where they stood.
There were no
other ladies in sight.
Suddenly the clear,

American voice broke through the man's barrier of silence.

"I know quite well what you are, you know. You may just as well tell me your name as leave me to find it out for myself."

He looked at her then for the first time, keenly, even critically. His clean-shaven mouth wore a very curious expression.

"My name is West," he said, after a moment.

She nodded briskly.

"Your professional name, I suppose. You are a professional, of course?"

His eyes continued to watch her narrowly. They were blue eyes, piercingly, icily blue.

"Why 'of course,' if one may ask?"

She laughed a light, sweet laugh, inexpressibly gay. Cynthia Mortimer could be charmingly inconsequent when she chose.

"I don't think you are a bit clever, you know," she said. "I knew what you were directly I saw you standing by the gangway watching the people coming on board. You looked really professional then, just as if you didn't care a red cent whether you caught your man or not. I knew you did care though, and I was ready to dance when I knew you hadn't got him. Think you'll track him down on our side?"

West turned his eyes once more upon the heaving, grey water, carelessly flicking the ash from his cigarette.

"I don't think," he said briefly. "I know."

"You—know?" The wide eyes opened wider, but they gathered no information from the unresponsive profile that smoked the cigarette. "You know where Mr. Nat Verney is?" she breathed, almost in a whisper. "You don't say! Then—then you weren't really watching out for him at the gangway?"

He jerked up his head with an enigmatical laugh.

"My methods are not so simple as that," he

said.

Cynthia joined quite generously in his laugh, notwithstanding its hard note of ridicule. She had become keenly interested in this man, in spite of—possibly in consequence of—the rebuffs he so unsparingly administered. She was not accustomed to rebuffs, this girl with her delicate, flower-like beauty. They held for her something of the charm of novelty, and abashed her not at all.

"And you really think you'll catch him?" she questioned, a note of honest regret in her voice.

"Don't you want him to be caught?"

He pitched his cigarette overboard and turned to her with less of churlishness in his bearing.

She met his eyes quite frankly.

"I should just love him to get away," she declared, with kindling eyes. "Oh, I know he's a regular sharper, and he's swindled heaps of people—I'm one of them, so I know a little about it. He swindled me out of five hundred dollars, and I can tell you I was mad at first. But now that he is flying from justice, I'm game enough to want him to get away. I suppose my sympathies generally lie with the hare, Mr. West. I'm sorry if it annoys you, but I was created that way."

West was frowning, but he smiled with some cynicism over her last remarks.

"Besides," she continued, "I couldn't help admiring him. He has a regular genius for swindling—that man. You'll agree with me there?"

A sudden heavy roll of the vessel pitched her forward before he could reply. He caught her round the waist, saving her from a headlong fall, and she clung to him, laughing like a child at the mishap.

"I think I'll have to go below," she decided regretfully. "But you've been good to me, and I'm glad I spoke. I've always been somewhat prejudiced against detectives till to-day. My cousin Archie—you saw him in the cardroom last night—vowed you were nothing half so interesting. Why is it, I wonder, that detectives always look like journalists?" She looked at him with eyes of friendly criticism. "You didn't deceive me, you see. But then"— ingenuously—"I'm clever in some ways, much more clever than you'd think. Now you won't cut me next time we meet, will you? Because—perhaps—I'm going to ask you to do something for me."

"What do you want me to do?"

The man's voice was hard, his eyes cold as steel, but his question had in it a shade—just a shade—of something warmer than mere curiosity.

She took him into her confidence without an instant's hesitation.

"My cousin Archie—you may have noticed—you were looking on last night—he's a very careless player, and headstrong too. But he can't afford to lose any, and I don't want him to come to grief. You see, I'm rather fond of him."

"Well?"

The man's brows were drawn down over his eyes. His expression was not encouraging.

"Well," she proceeded, undismayed, "I saw

you looking on, and you looked as if you knew a few things. So I thought you'd be a safe person to ask. I can't look after him; and his mother—well, she's worse than useless. But a man—a real strong man like you—is different. If I were to introduce you, couldn't you look after him a bit—just till we get across?"

With much simplicity she made her request, but there was a tinge of anxiety in her eyes. Certainly West, staring steadily forth over the grey waste of tumbling waters, looked sufficiently forbidding.

After several seconds of silence he flung an abrupt question:

"Why don't you ask some one else?"

"There is no one else," she answered.

"No one else?" He made a gesture of impatient incredulity.

"No one that I can trust," she explained.

"And you trust me?"

"Of course I do."

"Why?" Again he looked at her with a piercing scrutiny. His eyes held a savage, almost a threatening expression.

But the girl only laughed, lightly and confidently.

"Why? Oh, just because you are trustworthy, I guess. I can't think of any other reason."

West's look relaxed, became abstracted, and finally fell away from her.

"You appear to be a lady of some discernment," he observed drily.

She proffered her hand impulsively, her eyes dancing.

"My, that's the first pretty thing you've

said to me!" she declared flippantly. "I just like you, Mr. West!"

West was feeling for his cigarette case. He gave her his hand without looking at her, as if her approbation did not greatly gratify him. When she was gone he moved away along the wind-swept deck with his collar up to his ears and his head bent to the gale. His conversation with the American girl had not apparently made him feel any more sociably inclined towards his fellow-passengers.

Certainly, as Cynthia had declared, young Archibald Bathurst was an exceedingly reckless player. He lacked the judgment and the cool brain essential to a good cardplayer, with the result that he lost much more often than he won. But notwithstanding this fact he had a passion for cards which no amount of defeat could abate—a passion which he never failed to indulge whenever an opportunity presented itself.

At the very moment when his cousin was making her petition on his behalf to the surly Englishman on deck, he was seated in the saloon with three or four men older than himself, playing and losing, playing and losing, with almost unvarying monotony, yet with a feverish relish that had in it something tragic.

He was only three-and-twenty, and, as he was wont to remark, ill-luck dogged him persistently at every turn. He never blamed himself when rash speculations failed, and he never profited by bitter experience. Simply, he was by nature a spendthrift, high-spirited, impulsive, weak, with little thought for the future and none at all for the past. Wherever he went he was popular. His gaiety and spontaneity won him favour. But no one took him very seriously. No one ever dreamed that his ill-luck was a cause for anything but mirth.

A good deal of money had changed hands when the party separated to dine, but, though young Bathurst was as usual a loser, he displayed no depression. Only, as he sauntered away to his cabin, he flung a laughing challenge to those who remained:

"See if I don't turn the tables presently!"

They laughed with him, pursuing him with chaff till he was out

of hearing. The boy
was a game youngster,
and he knew how to
lose. Moreover, it was
generally believed
that he could afford to
pay for his pleasures.

But a man who
met him suddenly
outside his cabin read
something other than
indifference upon
his flushed face. He
only saw him for an
instant. The next,

Archie had swung past and was gone, a clanging door shutting him from sight.

When the little knot of cardplayers reassembled after dinner their number was augmented. A short, broad-shouldered man, clean-shaven, with piercing blue eyes, had scraped acquaintance with one of them, and had accepted an invitation to join the play. Some surprise was felt among the rest, for this man had till then been disposed to hold aloof from his fellow-passengers, preferring a solitary cigarette to any amusements that might be going forward.

A New York man named Rudd muttered

to his neighbour that
the fellow might be
all right, but he had
the eyes of a sharper.
The neighbour in
response murmured
the words "private
detective" and Rudd
was relieved.

Archie Bathurst was
the last to arrive,
and dropped into the
place he had occupied
all the afternoon.
It was immediately

facing the stranger, whom he favoured with a brief and somewhat disparaging stare before settling down to play.

The game was a pure gamble. They played swiftly, and in silence. West seemed to take but slight interest in the issue, but he won steadily and surely. Young Bathurst, playing feverishly, lost and lost, and lost again. The fortunes of the other four players varied. But always the newcomer won his ventures.

The evening was half over when Archie suddenly and loudly demanded higher stakes, to turn his luck, as he expressed it.

"Double them if you

like," said West.

Rudd looked at him with a distrustful eye, and said nothing. The other players were disposed to accede to the boy's vehement request, and after a little discussion the matter was settled to his satisfaction. The game was resumed at higher points.

Some onlookers had

drawn round the table scenting excitement. Archie, sitting with his back to the wall, was playing with headlong recklessness. For a while he continued to lose, and then suddenly and most unexpectedly he began to win. A most rash speculation resulted in his favour, and from that moment it seemed that his luck had turned. Once or twice he lost, but these occasions were far outbalanced by several brilliant coups. The tide had turned at last in his favour.

He played as a man possessed, swiftly and feverishly. It seemed that he and West were to divide the honours. For West's luck scarcely varied, and Rudd continued to look at him askance.

For the greater part of an hour young Bathurst won with scarcely a break, till the spectators began to chaff him upon his outrageous success.

"You'd better stop," one man warned him. "She's a fickle jade, you know, Bathurst. Take too much for granted, and she'll desert you."

But Bathurst did not even seem to hear. He played with lowered eyes and twitching mouth, and his hands shook perceptibly. The gambler's lust was upon him.

"He'll go on all night," murmured the onlookers.

But this prophecy was

not to be fulfilled.

It was a very small thing that stemmed the racing current of the boy's success—no more than a slight click audible only to a few, and the tinkle of something falling—but in an instant, swift as a thunderbolt, the wings of tragedy swept down upon the little party gathered about the table.

Young Bathurst uttered a queer, half-choked exclamation, and dived downwards. But the man next to him, an Englishman named Norton, dived also, and it was he who, after a moment, righted himself with something shining in his hand which he proceeded grimly to display to the whole assembled company.

It was a small, folding mirror—little more than a toy, it looked— with a pin attached to its leathern back.

Deliberately Norton turned it over, examining it in such a way that others might examine it too. Then, having concluded his investigation of this very simple contrivance, he slapped it down upon the table with a gesture of unutterable contempt.

"The secret of success," he observed.

Every one present looked at Archie, who had sunk back in his chair white to the lips. He seemed to be trying to say something, but nothing came of it.

And then, quite calmly, ending a silence more terrible than any tumult of words, another voice made itself heard.

"Even so, Mr. Norton." West bent forward and with the utmost composure possessed himself of the shining thing upon the table. "This is my property. I have been rooking you fellows all the evening."

The avowal was so astounding and made with such complete sang-froid that no one uttered a word. Only every one turned from Archie to stare at the man who thus serenely claimed his own.

He proceeded with unvarying coolness to explain himself.

"It was really done as an experiment," he said. "I am not a card-sharper by profession, as some of you already know. But in the course of certain investigations not connected with the matter I now have in hand, I picked this thing up, and, being something of a specialist in certain forms of cheating, I made up my mind to try my hand at this and prove for myself its extreme simplicity. You see how easy it is to swindle, gentlemen, and the danger to which you expose yourselves. There is no necessity for me to explain the trick further. The instrument speaks for itself. It is merely a matter of dexterity, and keeping it out of sight."

He held it up
a second time
before his amazed
audience, twisted it
this way and that,
with the air of a
conjurer displaying
his smartest trick,
attached it finally to
the lapel of his coat,
and rose.

"As a practical
demonstration it
seems to have
acted very well," he

remarked. "And no harm done. If you are all satisfied, so am I."

He collected the notes at his elbow with a single careless sweep of the hand, and tossed them into the middle of the table; then, with a brief, collective bow, he turned to go. But Rudd, the first to recover from his amazement, sprang impetuously to his feet. "One moment, sir!" he said.

West stopped at once, a cold glint of humour in his eyes. Without a sign of perturbation he faced round, meeting the American's hostile scrutiny calmly, judicially.

"I wish to say," said Rudd, "on behalf of

myself, and—I think
I may take it—on
behalf of these other
gentlemen also, that
your action was a
most dastardly piece
of impertinence, to
give it its tamest
name. Naturally, we
don't expect Court
manners from one
of your profession,
but we do look for
ordinary common
honesty. But it seems
that we look in vain.

You have behaved like a mighty fine skunk, sir. And if you don't see that there's any crying need for a very humble apology, you've got about the thickest hide that ever frayed a horsewhip."

Every one was standing by the time this elaborate threat was uttered, and it was quite obvious that Rudd voiced the general opinion. The only one whose face expressed no indignation was Archie Bathurst. He was leaning against the wall, mopping his forehead with a shaking hand.

No one looked at him. All attention was centred upon West, who met it with a calm serenity suggestive of contempt. He showed himself in no hurry to respond to Rudd's indictment, and when he did it was not exclusively to Rudd that he spoke.

"I am sorry," he coolly said, "that you consider yourselves aggrieved by my experiment. I do not myself see in what way I have injured you. However, perhaps you are the best judges of that. If you consider an apology due to you, I am quite ready to apologise."

His glance rested for a second upon Archie, then slowly swept the entire assembly. There was scant humility about him, apologise though he might.

Rudd returned his look

with open disgust.
But it was Norton who
replied to West's calm
defence of himself.

"It is Bathurst who is
the greatest loser,"
he said, with a glance
at that young man,
who was beginning
to recover from his
agitation. "It was a
tom-fool trick to play,
but it's done. You
won't get another
opportunity for your

experiments on board this boat. So—if Bathurst is satisfied—I should say the sooner you apologise and clear out the better."

"We will confiscate this, anyway," declared Rudd, plucking the mirror from West's coat.

He flung it down, and ground his heel upon it with venomous

intention. West merely shrugged his shoulders.

"I apologise," he said briefly, "singly and collectively, to all concerned in my experiment, especially"—he made a slight pause—"to Mr. Bathurst, whose run of luck I deeply regret to have curtailed. If Mr. Bathurst is satisfied, I will now withdraw."

He paused again, as
if to give Bathurst
an opportunity to
express an opinion.
But Archie said
nothing whatever. He
was staring down upon
the table, and did not
so much as raise his
eyes.

West shrugged his
shoulders again, ever
so slightly, and swung

slowly upon his heel. In a dead silence he walked away down the saloon. No one spoke till he had gone.

A black, moaning night had succeeded the grey, gusty day. The darkness came down upon the sea like a pall, covering the long, heaving swell from sight—a darkness that wrapped close, such a darkness as could be felt—through which the spray drove blindly.

There was small attraction for passengers on deck, and West grimaced to himself as he emerged from the heated cabins. Yet it was not altogether distasteful to him. He was a man to whom a calm atmosphere meant intolerable stagnation. He was essentially born to fight his way in the world.

For a while he paced alone, to and fro, along the deserted deck, his hands behind him, the inevitable cigarette between his lips. But presently he paused and stood still close to the companion by which he had ascended. It was sheltered here, and he leaned against the woodwork by which Cynthia Mortimer had supported herself that morning, and smoked serenely and meditatively.

Minutes passed. There came the sound of hurrying feet upon the stairs behind him, and he moved a little to one side, glancing downwards.

The light at
the head of the
companion revealed
a man ascending,
bareheaded, and
in evening dress.
His face, upturned,
gleamed deathly
white. It was the face
of Archie Bathurst.

West suddenly
squared his shoulders

and blocked the opening.

"Go and get an overcoat, you young fool!" he said.

Archie gave a great start, stood a second, then, without a word, turned back and disappeared.

West left his sheltered corner and paced forward across

the deck. He came to a stand by the rail, gazing outwards into the restless darkness. There seemed to be the hint of a smile in his intent eyes.

A few more minutes drifted away. Then there fell a step behind him; a hand touched his arm.

"Can I speak to you?" Archie asked.

Slowly West turned.

"If you have anything of importance to say," he said.

Archie faced him with a desperate resolution.

"I want to ask you—I want to know—what in thunder you did it for!"

"Eh?" said West. "Did what?"

He almost drawled the words, as if to give the boy time to control his agitation.

Archie stared at him incredulously.

"You must know what I mean."

"Haven't an idea."

There was just a tinge of contempt this time in the words. What an unconscionable bungler the fellow was!

"But you must!" persisted Archie, blundering wildly. "I suppose you knew what you were doing just now when—when——"

"I generally know what I am doing," observed West.

"Then why——"

Archie stumbled again, and fell silent, as if he had hurt himself.

"I don't always care to discuss my motives," said West very decidedly.

"But surely—" Archie suddenly pulled up, realising that by this spasmodic method he was making no headway. "Look here, sir," he said, more quietly, "you've done a big thing for me to-night—a dashed fine thing! Heaven only knows what you did it for, but——"

"I have done nothing whatever for you," said West shortly. "You make a mistake."

"But you'll admit——"

"I admit nothing."

He made as if he would turn on his heel, but Archie caught him by the arm.

"I know I'm a cur," he said. And his voice shook a little. "I don't wonder you won't speak to me. But there are some things that can't be left unsaid. I'm going down now, at once, to tell those fellows what actually happened."

"Then you are going to make a big fool of yourself to no purpose," said West.

He stood still, scanning the boy's face with pitiless eyes. Archie writhed impotently.

"I can't stand it!" he

said, with vehemence. "I thought I was blackguard enough to let you do it. But— no doubt I'm a fool, as you say—I find I can't."

"You can't help yourself," said West. He planted himself squarely in front of Archie. "Listen to this!" he said. "You know what I am?"

"They say you are a detective," said Archie.

West nodded.

"Exactly. And, as such, I do whatever suits my purpose without explaining why to the rest of the world. If you are fortunate enough to glean a little advantage from what I do, take it, and be quiet about it. Don't hamper me with your acknowledgments. I assure you I have no more concern for your ultimate fate than those fellows below that you've been swindling all the evening. One thing I will say, though, for your express benefit. You will never make a good, even an indifferently good, gambler. And as to card-sharping, you've no talent whatever. Better give it up."

His blue eyes looked straight at Archie with a stare that was openly supercilious, and Archie stood abashed.

"You—you are awfully good," he stammered at length.

West's brief laugh

lived in his memory for long after. It held an indescribable sting, almost as if the man resented something. Yet the next moment unexpectedly he held out his hand.

"A matter of opinion," he observed drily. "Good-night! Remember what I have said to you."

"I shall never forget

it," Archie said earnestly.

He wrung the extended hand hard, waited an instant, then, as West turned from him with that slight characteristic lift of the shoulders, he moved away and went below.

"I'd just like a little talk with you, Mr. West, if I may." Lightly the audacious voice arrested him, and, as it were, against his will, West stood still.

She was standing behind him in the morning sunshine, her hair blown all about her face, her grey eyes wide and daring, full of an alert friendliness that could not be ignored. She moved forward with her light, free step and stood beside him. West was smoking as usual. His expression was decidedly surly. Cynthia glanced at him once or twice before she spoke.

"You mustn't mind what I'm going to ask you," she said at length gently. "Now, Mr. West, what was it—exactly—that happened in the saloon last night?

Surely you'll tell me by myself if I promise—honest Injun—not to tell again."

"Why should I tell you?" said West, in his brief, unfriendly style.

Cynthia was undaunted. "Because you're a gentleman," she said boldly.

He shrugged his shoulders. "I don't know what reason I have given you to say so."

"No?" She looked at him with a funny little smile. "Well then, I just feel it in my bones; and nothing you do or leave undone will make me believe the contrary."

"Much obliged to you,"

said West. His blue eyes were staring straight out over the sea to the long, blue sky-line. He seemed too absorbed in what he saw to pay much attention to the girl beside him.

But she was not to be shaken off. "Mr. West," she began again, breaking in upon his silence, "do you know what they are saying about you to-day?"

"Haven't an idea."

"No," she said. "And I don't suppose you care either. But I care. It matters a lot to me."

"Don't see how," threw in West.

He turned in his abrupt, disconcerting way, and gave her a

piercing look. She averted her face instantly, but he had caught her unawares.

"Good heavens!" he said. "What's the matter?"

"Nothing," she returned, with a sort of choked vehemence. "There's nothing the matter with me. Only I'm feeling badly about—about what

I asked you to do yesterday. I'd sooner have lost every dollar I have in the world, if I had only known, than—than have you do—what you did."

"Good heavens!" West said again.

He waited a little then, looking down at her as she leaned upon the rail with downcast face. At length, as she did not raise her head, he addressed her for the first time on his own initiative:

"Miss Mortimer!"

She made a slight movement to indicate that she was listening, but she remained gazing down into the green and white of the racing water.

Unconsciously he moved a little nearer to her. "There is no occasion for you to feel badly," he said. "I had my own reasons for what I did. It doesn't much matter what they were. But let me tell you for your comfort that neither socially nor professionally has it done me any harm."

"They are all saying:

'Set a thief to catch a thief,'" she interposed, with something like a sob in her voice.

"They can say what they like."

West's tone expressed the most stoical indifference, but she would not be comforted.

"If only I

hadn't—asked you to!" she murmured.

He made his peculiar, shrugging gesture. "What does it matter? Moreover, what you asked of me was something quite apart from this. It had nothing whatever to do with it."

She stood up sharply at that, and faced him with burning

eyes. "Oh, don't tell me that lie!" she exclaimed passionately. "I'm not such a child as to be taken in by it. You don't deceive me at all, Mr. West. I know as well as you do—better—that the man who did the swindling last night was not you. And I'm sick—I'm downright sick—whenever I think of it!"

West's expression changed slightly as he looked at her. He seemed to regard her as a doctor regards the patient for whom he contemplates a change of treatment.

"See here," he abruptly said. "You are distressing yourself all to no purpose. If you will promise to keep it secret, I'll tell you the facts of the case."

Cynthia's face changed also. She caught eagerly at the suggestion. "Yes?" she said. "Yes? I promise, of course. And I'm quite trustworthy."

"I believe you are," he said, with a grim smile. "Well, the fact of the matter is this. The man we want is on board this ship, but being only a private detective, I don't possess a warrant for his arrest. Therefore all I can do is to keep him in sight. And I can only do that by throwing him as far as possible off the scent. If he takes me for a card-sharper, all the better. For he's as slippery as an eel, and I have to play him pretty carefully."

He ceased. Cynthia's

eyes were growing wider and wider.

"Nat Verney on board this ship?" she gasped.

He nodded.

"Yes. You wanted him to get away, didn't you? But I don't think he will, this time. He will probably be arrested directly we reach New York.

But, meantime, I must watch out."

"Oh!" breathed Cynthia. "Then"—with sudden hope dawning in her eyes—"it really was your doing, that trick at the card-table last night?"

West uttered his brief, hard laugh.

"What do you take me for?"

She heaved a great sigh of relief.

"And it wasn't Archie, after all? I'm thankful you told me. I thought—I thought— But it doesn't matter, does it? Tell me, do tell me, Mr. West," drawing very close to him, "which—which is Mr. Nat Verney?"

West seemed to hesitate.

"Oh, do tell me!" she begged. "I know I'm only a woman, but I always keep my word. And it's only two days more to New York."

He looked closely into her eyes and yielded.

"I'm trusting you with my reputation," he said. "It's the stout, red-faced man called Rudd."

"Mr. Rudd?" She started back. "You don't say? That man?" There followed a short pause while she digested the information. Then, as on the previous morning, she suddenly extended her hand. "Well, I hate that man, anyway. And I believe you're really clever. If you like, Mr. West, I'll help you to watch out."

"Thanks!" said West. He took the little hand into a tight grip, still looking straight into her eyes. There was a light in his own that shone like a blue flame. "Thanks!" he said again, as he released it. "You're very good, Miss Mortimer. But you mustn't be seen with me, you know. You've got to remember that I'm a swindler."

The girl laughed aloud. It pleased her to feel that this taciturn man had taken her into his confidence at last. "I shall remember," she said lightly.

And she went away, not only comforted, but gay of heart.

During the remainder of the voyage, West was treated with

extreme coolness by every one. It did not seem to abash him in the least. He came and went in the crowd with the utmost sang-froid, always preoccupied, always self-contained. Cynthia observed him from a distance with admiration. The man had taken her fancy. She was keenly interested in his methods, as well as in his decidedly unusual personality. She observed Rudd also, and noted the obvious suspicion with which he regarded West. On the night before their arrival she saw the latter alone for a moment, and whispered to him that Mr. Rudd seemed uneasy. At which information West merely laughed sardonically. He was holding a small parcel, to which, after a moment, he drew her attention.

"I was going to ask you to accept this," he said. "It is nothing very important, but I should like you to have it. Don't open it before to-morrow."

"What is it?" asked Cynthia, in surprise.

He frowned in his abrupt way.

"It doesn't matter; something connected with my profession. I shouldn't give it you, if I didn't know you were to be trusted."

"But—but"—she hesitated a little—"ought I to take it?"

He raised his shoulders.

"I shall give it to the captain for you, if you don't. But I would rather give it to you direct."

In face of this, Cynthia yielded, feeling as if he compelled her.

"But mayn't I open it?"

"No." West's eyes held hers for a second. "Not till to-morrow.

And, in case we don't meet again, I'll say good-bye."

"But we shall meet in New York?" she urged, with a sudden sense of loss. "Or perhaps in Boston? My father would really like to meet you."

"Much obliged," said West, with his grim smile. "But I'm not much of a society man. And I don't think I shall find myself in Boston at present."

"Then—then—I sha'n't see you again—ever?" Cynthia's tone was unconsciously tragic. Till that moment she had scarcely realised how curiously strong an attraction this man held for her.

West's expression changed. His

emotionless blue eyes became suddenly more blue, and intense with a vital fire. He leaned towards her as one on the verge of vehement speech.

Then abruptly his look went beyond her, and he checked himself.

"Who knows?" he said carelessly. "Good-bye

for the present, anyway! It's been a pleasant voyage."

He straightened himself with the words, nodded, and turned aside without so much as touching her hand.

And Cynthia, glancing round with an instinctive feeling of discomfiture, saw Rudd with another man, standing watching them at the end of the passage.

In the dark of early morning they reached New York. Most of the passengers decided to remain on board for breakfast, which was served at an early hour in the midst of a hubbub and turmoil indescribable.

Cynthia, with her aunt

and Archie, partook of a hurried meal in the thick of the ever-shifting crowd. She looked in vain for West, her grey eyes searching perpetually.

One friend after another came up to bid them good-bye, stood a little, talking, and presently drifted away. The whole ship from end to end hummed like a hive of bees.

She was glad when at
length she was able
to escape from the
noisy saloon. She had
not slept well, and
her nerves were on
edge. The memory
of that interrupted
conversation
with West, of the
confidence unspoken,
went with her
continually. She had
an almost feverish

longing to see him once more, even though it were in the heart of the crowd. He had been about to tell her something. Of that she was certain. She had an intense, an almost passionate desire to know what it was. Surely he would not—he could not—go ashore without seeing her again!

She had not intended

to open the packet he had given her till she was ashore herself, but a palpitating curiosity tugged ever at her resolution till at length she could resist it no longer. West was nowhere to be seen, and she felt she must know more. It was intolerable to be thus left in the dark. Through the scurrying multitude of departing passengers, she began to make her way back to her cabin. Her progress was of necessity slow, and once in a crowded corner she was stopped altogether.

Two men were talking together close to her. Their backs were towards her, and in the general confusion they did not observe her futile impatience to pass.

"Oh, I knew the fellow was a wrong 'un, all along," were the first words that filtered to the girl's consciousness as she stood. "But I didn't think he was responsible for that card trick, I must say. Young Bathurst looked so abominably hangdog."

It was the Englishman, Norton,

who spoke, and the man who stood with him was Rudd. Cynthia realised the near presence of the latter with a sensation of disgust. His drawling tones grated upon her intolerably.

"Waal," he said, "it was just that card trick that opened my eyes—I shouldn't have noticed him, otherwise. I knew that young Bathurst was square. He hasn't the brains to be anything else. And when this chap butted in with his thick-ribbed impudence, I guessed right then that we hadn't got a beginner to deal with. After that I watched for a bit, and there were several little things that made me begin to reflect. So the next evening I got a wireless message off to my partner in New York, and I reckon that did the trick. When we came up alongside this morning, the vultures were all ready for him. I took them to his cabin myself. There was no fuss at all. He saw it was all up, and gave in without a murmur. They were only just in time, though. In another thirty seconds, he would have been off. It was a clever piece of work, I flatter myself, to net Mr. Nat Verney so neatly."

The Englishman began to laugh, but suddenly broke off short as a girl's face, white and quivering, came between them.

"Who is this man?" the high, breathless

voice demanded. "Which—which is Mr. Nat Verney?"

Rudd looked down at her through narrowed eyes. He was smiling—a small, bitter smile.

"Waal, Miss Mortimer," he began, "I reckon you have first right to know——"

She turned from him

imperiously.

"You tell me," she commanded Norton.

Norton looked genuinely uncomfortable, and, probably in consequence, he answered her with a gruffness that sounded brutal.

"It was West. He has been arrested. His

own fault entirely. No one would have suspected him if he hadn't been a fool, and given his own show away."

"He wasn't a fool!" Cynthia flashed back fiercely. "He was my friend!"

"I shouldn't be in too great a hurry to claim that distinction," remarked Rudd. "He's about the best-known rascal in the two hemispheres."

But Cynthia did not wait to hear him. She had slipped past, and was gone.

In her own cabin at last, she bolted the door and tore open that packet connected with his profession which he had given her the night before. It contained a roll of notes to the value of a hundred pounds, wrapped in a sheet of notepaper on which was scrawled a single line: "With apologies from the man who swindled you."

There was no signature of any sort. None was needed! When Cynthia finally left her cabin an hour later, her eyes were bright with that brightness which comes from the shedding of many tears.

THE END

ABOUT THE AUTHOR

Ethel M. Dell has delighted millions around the world with her best selling stories of love and longing. A shy and private person, she was forty when she married the love her life, a solider named Gerald Tahourdin Savage. She first published The Swindler in 1923.

ABOUT THE COVER

The cover is adapted from a poster for the 1941 movie, "Meet John Doe," starring Gary Cooper and Barbara Stanwyck.

* The Lady Rustic *
Alexander Pushkin
Her father hated their neighbors, but she wanted to meet the young man next door. So she hatched a plan to catch her man. But what if that's the easy part?

* Letters of a Woman Homesteader *
Elinore Pruitt Stewart
Memoir of a widowed mother on the frontier.

MORE BOOKS AT:
superlargeprint.com

KEEP ON READING!

This book is set in a font designed by
Abelardo Gonzalez called OpenDyslexic.

ISBN 1979568693
ISBN 978-1979568692

Printed in Great Britain
by Amazon

30417548R00079